A Royal Payne

By Pixie Chica

Copyright

Thank You!

Thank you for your purchase of My Royal Payne.   I hope you enjoy the story and will consider leaving a review or telling a friend about the book. I love hearing from readers! To keep in touch and follow my news, please visit me on facebook.
facebook.com/pixiechicaauthor

A Royal Payne
by
Pixie Chica

Cameron Harley

I left my life in Small Town USA for a dream job in an exotic country. My life was going to be fabulous. Only...it didn't quite turn out that way. Five years later, I'm not only stuck working crazy hours as an executive assistant, but I have a hot and cold boss. Queen Helena Payne. The Royal Pain in my A... You get the picture. This is my life day in, day out, until one call changes everything.

I'm heading back home. Even if I'm madly in love with her. It's time I set my sights on reality...like someone who actually sees me as more than the help.

Queen Helena Payne

She thinks I don't see her, but there's nothing further from the truth. I see every inch of her, and I love riling her up just to see her storm off. She's my assistant, the best one that's ever existed. She's also off-limits. As the queen of my country, there are expectations about who I should marry. Cameron Harley is not it.

I may not be able to touch, but I can watch. I'll keep her by my side for as long as I can. Only it seems my time is up. Now, I'm on a wild goose chase after the one I can't let go.

Dedication

This one goes out to everyone.
Surviving 2020 deserves a dedication.
I can't believe it's only April.

Chapter One

~ Cameron ~

"Did you fix—"

"The date for the duke to come by? Yes, already changed it in your calendars as well as called his PR Manager about photo ops," I blurt out.

"What about my paren—?" she tries again, but I'm too quick.

"Told them you were recovering from a horrible cold," I interject. "They're staying away." Moving over to the side of her enormous desk, I reach for the filing cabinet. I pull out the pink file. Thankfully, I had the bright idea to color coordinate everything years ago. It's proved invaluable in time crunches like today.

"Good, good. The—"

"Right here. I'll be leaving for lunch now," I inform her. "I've ordered yours. It should be up any minute." I open the file to the page Helena will be working on for the next three hours.

"Turkey on rye, two oranges, and a black coffee with two Splendas. I added a bottle of water because your doctor said you need to stay hydrated."

Queen Helena finally looks up at me, her mouth turning up at the sides, baring her perfect pearly whites. "Always two steps ahead aren't you, Cam-Cam?"

"With the amount of work, you have me doing, two steps ahead means I'm ten steps behind at any given time," I reply, stretching over her to reach the top shelf of her desk.

She stands, startling me as she closes in from behind. Her taller frame towers over my own by a few inches, the subtle scent of her lavender and jasmine perfume hitting me. My breath catches at the proximity. She proceeds to lean forward, and I feel the heat from her warm body at my back. *Fuck, too close.*

"What's the matter, Cameron?" she whispers against my ear.

Shivers run up my body that always reacts this way to her. She knows what she's doing. It's a little game she loves to play. See how far she can push before I demand she back up.

As with every other time she gets this close, I get a bit lightheaded. My attraction for her is unmistakable. After working so closely together,

I've broken the capital rule. Don't fall in love with your boss. But that's exactly what I've done. Now, I'm in the ninth level of hell because of this attraction. The fact that, most days, I also want to kill her is the tenth. But her lack of respect for personal space is the icing on the proverbial inferno cake.

"I asked you a question," she demands her tone low as her hand grazes my wrist.

"I know," I murmur unable to form another word. If I do, I might trip up and finally say something I won't be able to take back. I swallow hard, looking anywhere but at her, my resistance slowly fading.

For a moment, we both stay in this position. Her question goes unanswered, and I don't dare move. It's moments like these I feel there's a connection between us. An imaginary hope that makes my heart skip a beat. I let my fantasy wander, if only for a second. Maybe this time, she won't back away. Or worse, she'll end this torturous moment as if it's a joke that proves how easily she can provoke a response from me. For just a moment, I don't have to acknowledge this is a cruel hoax she plays against me, knowing full well I'm the one she takes out her curiosity on.

"Well?" Her thumb grazes my pulse point.

I have to stop this now. Clearing my throat, I break the spell. "Well what?"

I pull the binder I'm looking for and try to move. Her hand wraps around my forearm keeping me hostage. This isn't good. I need to find a way out. Gathering all the strength I can, I pull her hand off me, smirking at her.

"I'm just peachy. Are you okay?"

"Yup. Just peachy, too. As you Americans say. Such an odd use of the English language. You even get a bit of…what's it called?" she mocks, straightening herself. "Oh yeah, twang."

"I don't have a twang, but bless your heart." I grin, placing my hand over my heart and batting my eyelashes.

"Aw, that used to be a lot cuter when I didn't know what it meant." She sits back down and sighs. Once again, unamused and ready to keep working the day away, she opens the pink file and reads. She's shutting me out again, her temperament going from hot to cold in a matter of seconds.

I'm grabbing my bag from the floor when Lorenzo, our lead security guard, comes flying in.

"The queen is here," he says in a weird whisper-shout.

"Of course, I am."

"No, the other queen. Your mom!" he exclaims, before backing out the door again.

"Fuck! Stall her!" she demands right before the door closes. Then she turns to me. "I thought you took care of this," she murmurs through gritted teeth.

"I did, but maybe, you should listen to me when I tell you not to avoid your mother for a whole month."

Her tactic for attack not working, she moves to empathy. Her whole face transforms giving me her best puppy eyes, and I almost feel sorry for her, but given that it's Marion Payne who's arrived, I'm out.

"Help me!"

"Nope, you're on your own with that one." I blow a kiss to her just as the door opens, earning me a scowl from Satan's spawn.

I greet the woman, but as always, she doesn't bother to glance my way. Instead, she takes her seat in front of Helena's desk. Dramatically falling into her chair as if it was the royal way to do so. Sitting there, with her overly tanned skin and mink coat, she looks more like a stuffed potato than the ex-queen. Rolling my eyes, I close the door behind me.

The woman is a horror, something I found out the very first day I came to work here. Back then, I was a fresh-out-of-college twenty-two-year-old from the middle of nowhere USA. I'd arrived at the castle with the clothes on my back and two-hundred bucks that would barely get me a room for the night. Having already secured the job before taking the plane trip over here, I was ecstatic. That lasted all of ten minutes. Marion Payne had approached me with a crocodile smile as I left Lorenzo's office.

"Oh, you must be the new stable girl," she'd said, looking me over from the bottom up. I'd quickly corrected her, informing her I was the new Executive Assistant to the queen. Her tone condescending, she'd told me I reminded her of Jack, their often dirty but efficient foreman. All I could do was bite my tongue. Considering I was in a foreign country and at the mercy of its government, I knew better than to speak back. But as the Lord as my witness, that woman could make a preacher cuss. At a loss for words from her insult, I'd walked away, mentally giving her my two middle fingers.

Since then, I try my best to avoid her. That isn't hard since Helena barely sees her to begin with. Unfortunately, impromptu visits like today always messes my boss up. She'll be stuck in there for two-to-four hours, depending on how long her father was out golfing, and afterwards, she'll be in a foul mood.

I prepare myself for the hell to come, including the extra hours I'll have to pull tonight, to make up for the visit. It's the hardest part of being the assistant to a woman who runs a whole kingdom—lack of down time. Most days, I pull sixteen hours shifts, only taking one day off a week. Even then, I'm often on-call most of the day.

Entering the kitchen, I wave to Delci, who comes over with the lunch I called down. The knowing look on her face is hard to miss as she places my warm clam chowder and grilled cheese before me. I keep my eyes on the kitchen island, not ready for another lecture on the importance of a meal I don't inhale. Unfortunately, that's never been a deterrent before.

"What is it now?"

"Don't really have time to talk about it, Delci."

"She'll work you to the bone. You're thinning away to nothing," she says pinching my arm between her fingers. "You've lost over thirty pounds since you came to work here."

"Now, you're just exaggerating, and you know it," I argue. While I've lost a few pounds from often forgetting to eat, it's nowhere near thirty pounds.

"Stop lying to yourself, my dear. You know very well Adeline keeps having to take your clothes in."

"Fine, fine, I lost a couple pounds. I'll sit here and eat this lunch without interruptions if you —"

The *Sweet Home Alabama* ringtone interrupts our conversation as my sister, Marni's number flashes across the screen. I hold up a finger to Delci, excusing myself to take this call. Leaving my shoes in the kitchen, I go barefoot to the side hall reserved for the dining staff. At this hour, no one is around, and it gives me the privacy I need. Fear creeps up my body as I answer the call, wondering why my little sister is calling. I have a standing phone date with them, so this is out of the norm.

"Yello," I greet her as always.

"Oh, thank God! I wasn't sure you'd pick up since you're always so busy around this hour," she shrieks from the other side of the line.

The sound of a celebration in the background hits me in the middle of my chest. I distinctly hear my uncle Joe hollering *Red Solo Cup* louder than the

Toby Keith song blaring through the radio. I can picture it perfectly from here. He's probably had one too many, my Aunt Paula hoping to stop him by threatening to withhold pleasures. My dad's sitting in his chair, getting a laugh at it all. Then there's Mama, who as the perfect hostess, is making sure drinks and food are plentiful. God, I miss them.

I used to be the life of all the parties, celebrating with the best of them. Being a Harley, through and through. What happened to me? Oh yeah, I wanted an adventure. The thought itself would be laughable, if it wasn't for how sad and pathetic my life actually turned out.

"Sis, you there?" Marni calls out to me, bringing me back to the here and now.

"Oh, yeah. Sorry. Everything okay? You don't usually call me on a Thursday afternoon."

"Where is your brain, Cameron? You know it's the middle of the night here!"

"Right, right. Sometimes, it slips my mind," I countered, sitting on the floor and tucking my feet underneath me. The pressure feels good on my sore feet. "Anyway, was there a reason for your call? I've got about ten minutes left of my lunch."

"Tell that boss of yours to shove it where the sun don't shine. She works you too hard. Besides, your ass will be on the next plane out of there!"

"Marni, are you drunk?" I ask, puzzled at her statement.

"Not a single drink. Okay, no, that's a lie. I had a couple shots, but that's beside the point. Cam, I'm getting married!" she yells, causing me to pull the phone away from my ear or risk damage. "Josh proposed tonight. I'm getting married this weekend. An Easter wedding, what could be sweeter?"

"Whoa, Marni, that's not enough time to plan a wedding. I can't just up and leave here. I've got a busy schedule for the next two weeks."

"Well, I don't know. Figure it out, Cam. I'm your only sister, and I need you as my maid of honor," she demands, her voice rising a few octaves. There's no way she's rescheduling. Marni Harley does as she pleases no matter what.

"Wait! Maid of honor? Really?" I squeal, realizing what a big deal this really is. My little sister is getting married, and here I am, trying to damper on her parade.

"See, you want to be part of this. Come on, sis. We all miss you. It's been five years. Five long years, let that sink in," she reasons with me. "Besides, I need a bachelorette party! One for the ages, the Harley sisters wreaking havoc on our small town."

That sounded like heaven right now. A whole week away from this place, where I spend day in and day out worrying about the next fire I need to extinguish. Memories of my carefree days at home, where all that mattered was having fun, play through my head like a beacon. I'm fucking doing this. Cameron Harley was taking a week off.

"I'm coming, baby sis. You tell that Josh boy of yours he better be ready. The Harley sisters are gonna paint the town red."

"Fuck, yeah, that's the Cam I know!" she celebrates on the other side of the phone before announcing to everyone I'm coming. Loud cheers erupt with various expletives being shouted in excitement. Hearing how happy they are about seeing me makes it hard to keep tears at bay. So many nights I've lain awake, second guessing if they even want to see me again. Their happiness squashes those fears.

I talk with my sister for a bit longer, while she goes through a list of must-haves. I stash away the information in my brain for the plane ride home. By the time I get to the ranch, I'll have half of it done. Looking down at my watch, I realize I've overextended my lunch break.

"Fuck, Marni, I got to go. Helena will kill me. I'm supposed to be done with the calls about the palace's Easter dinner as of twenty minutes ago."

"Fine, but you better be on a plane tomorrow," she warns.

"I promise. I wouldn't miss my best friend getting married. And Marni?"

"Yeah?"

"I'm very happy for you. Josh and you are made for one another. I love you."

"I love you too, sis."

Chapter Two

~ Helena ~

"Mother, for the hundredth time, I don't need to get married right now. Do not bring any of your so-called suitors to the Easter dinner," I growl out, having enough of this conversation.

"No one will take you seriously, Helena. I don't know why your father left you in charge. You have plenty of uncles who are more than happy to take the position," she snarls, impatiently tapping her nails on my desk.

I massage my temples, trying to ease the headache she's brought on. Every single time she comes to see me, it's to criticize my choices. From my clothes to the fact our kingdom is kingless. If she only knew just how kingless I plan to keep it. No amount of suitors can ever change my mind.

That's because of Cameron, my assistant. While I'll will never be able to cross that line, it doesn't change the fact my heart belongs to her. I'll remain faithful to her forever. She's the definition of perfect. Brains, beauty, a heart of gold, and a mouth that went from professional to smack talk in seconds. A mouth I want nothing more than to ravish.

"Helena, are you listening to me?" my mother snaps, whipping her cane against the wood of my desk.

"No, Mother, I'm not. I have a lot of work to do."

Needing a moment, I stand and walk to the window. "Why are you even here? You're supposed to be on vacation with father."

"I am on vacation. I came by to say hello and see how your fake cold is coming along. This is still my house. You're merely a guest until you find a husband who can rule it," she throws back, unhappy with my lack of amusement where her plans are concerned.

Fire courses hotter through my veins the more she speaks. I want her out, and right now. Pulling my cell phone from my pocket, I discreetly text Cameron to come save me. It goes unanswered for minutes that feel like hours. With each resend I push through, my annoyance level rises. I will have more than a few choice words for her when she finally answers. What is she doing anyway?

My phone vibrates after the fiftieth message, and I slide it open.

Cam-Cam: *I'm coming. Quit your griping!*

Not two seconds later, the soft knock comes followed by her peeking head through the doorway.

"Sorry to interrupt. Helena, there's an emergency with the Easter dinner. You need to call Lydia to go over some last-minute details that have gone awry," she says with fake concern.

"Isn't that what she pays you for? Seriously, Helena. If she's not good at her job, why do you keep her?" my mother complains, looking down at her manicured fingers.

"Mother, I have a crisis on my hands. Cameron is here to assist me, not make decisions for me. I have to make a call. You're welcome to stay, but you'll have to be quiet."

At my declaration, she shoots up from her seat, clearly uninterested in mundane tasks. A weight lifts from my shoulders when she walks away. I didn't think she'd ever leave.

Cameron waits for her at the door, opening it wide as she approaches it. Once she's gone, the latch is turned to give me privacy.

"Well, that was a quick visit."

"Not quick enough," I snap. "Where the hell have you been? When I text, you answer. That's how this works. Remember who ultimately pays you."

"What did you just say?"

"I don't have time for these little games you enjoy playing. Go bring me the menus for the Easter gathering. I need to go over everything, detail-by-detail. While you're out there, make sure you order us dinner. I don't want any interruptions. Try and actually move like you care about your job."

Cameron's cheeks are crimson red against her tanned skin. Both her hands are firmly on her hips while she stares me down, ready to tell me off. I've seen her mad, but I may have crossed the line this time. I should apologize. It's the logical thing to do, but the words are stuck in my throat. I'm not sorry for what I said. I'm pissed she wasn't around when I needed her. She's always supposed to answer when I call. It's her job.

"No." The single word falls from her lips like a dare, further provoking my ill mood. "As a matter of fact, I'll bring you the information you need. Then I'll call Mandy, my backup, and I'm leaving on vacation. Which is what I was coming to tell you."

"The hell you are!"

Silence falls upon the room. Our eyes lock, neither of us willing to back down. Whatever has gotten into her, better come right back out because there's no way I'm letting her leave on a vacation. Cameron belongs by my side, and what I say goes.

"You can't stop me. I'm well overdue one, and my little sister is getting married. I already got the approval from the employee agency. It's where I went when you kept buzzing me while your mother was visiting."

"It's not happening. I'll call down there myself and cancel it, if you won't. You work for me, not the employing agency. So go and fetch what I asked for, now!" I hiss, moving from the window and meeting her eye-to-eye.

"Fine, if that's what you think, then I'll quit. I refuse to miss my sister's wedding. I work hard here and give it my all. With everything I do for you, you should be understanding."

There's no lie in her eyes as she speaks. None of the usual glint that appears when we engage in our back-and-forth banter. She really means every word, and something inside me cracks.

"Then leave! I don't need you," I spit out. "There're plenty others who can do what you do. Probably better and cheaper."

I'm interrupted by a call on my landline, saving me from saying something I can truly regret.

My direct office number can only be reached by two people. Since it's not Cameron, it must be my father calling.

I run to pick it up. Of course, my father is concerned about my mother's visit not even half an hour ago. I try to calm him, assuring him she didn't understand me correctly when the door slams. Glancing over my shoulder, I curse. Cameron is gone.

"Father, I'm having some problems right now with staffing. I have to call you back," I plead with him. I need to find Cameron before she does something stupid like take me seriously. There's no getting off the phone with him, though.

* * * *

By the time I manage to get off the phone with my father, most of the afternoon is gone. His habit of rambling puts me further off schedule. Which doesn't bode well for me. He doesn't understand why I'm so busy, given he ruled very differently than I do. While some royals spend their time attending events and running their country from a less proactive stance, I don't. I'm on the front lines, dealing with all the day-to-day situations that come up. Jegan is a small country, a quarter of the size of Belgium, with a population of less than two million. Handling it is doable, but not without Cameron.

She's been with me from day one, hired the day after my coronation. Her angelic face showed up in my office in a pristine suit, ready to take on the world. She's so full of life and wonder, taking on every task with gusto. I fucked up, and I needed to fix this.

Forgetting about the dreaded timelines, I head to find her. I don't deserve someone as good as her in my life, but I want her in it. Always. Just as I want her by my side this weekend. Her company is the only way I can stay sane with all the guests scheduled to arrive.

My plan is quickly thwarted though, the darkened hallway that houses both my quarters and her room next to it warning me to not disturb. A feeling of dread overtakes me the closer I get to her door. I place my ear to it, but no sound comes from the other side. My fear deepens when I get no answer after banging on it a few times.

Where are you? You've never walked out before.

Placing my palms to the door, as if I'll magically feel her presence, I try to calm down. I'm probably psyching myself out, knowing she always turns the hall light off when she doesn't want to be disturbed. This is Cameron we're talking about. She wouldn't do anything rash. She may have even gone on a walk to clear her head. Although she enjoys them, she hasn't been able to take one as of late, since I keep demanding more and more of her time.

Logic wins, pushing the feeling away. I mouth a quiet, "I'm sorry," then head back to my office. I'll work alone for the day and give her the space she needs. Tomorrow, with things calm, I'll explain why she can't go. Everything will go back to normal.

Chapter Three

~ Cameron ~

I hold on to the armrests of my window seat as we prepare for landing. It's quite peculiar that with all the plane rides I've taken with Helena, I'm still so deathly afraid. In times like these, she'd hold my hand to distract me or say something absurd to piss me off. Those are her only settings, sweet or jackass. I guess jackass won out, after all.

Her last words to me were the final push I needed to open my eyes. I'd made up this fantasy for years about her and I. My only reason for staying was because I felt essential to her. I'd concocted this little fairytale where I was meant to cross paths with her. It was all bullshit my stupid heart believed.

How could I be so blind to think she felt something for me, too? She never saw me as anything other than a means to an end. But I couldn't help how I felt. Even now, so many miles apart, I wonder if she is okay? Will she survive the Easter dinner without me?

As the plane touches down on the runway, I know my pity party can't continue. It's time to forget about Helena. I'm no longer part of her world, and the sooner I assimilate that the better I'll fare. Soon, I'll be back home at Harley Ranch, restarting my life. It was the same mentality I had five years ago when I'd left home. I'd pulled the bandage right off, leaving all my family behind. Surely, I could do it again.

Granted, back then, I was fresh out of college with a business major and nowhere to go. I'd itched to see the world, explore, be everything my family wasn't. The departure wasn't a hardship.

It was for the best then. It will be for the best now.

It had to be, right?

* * * *

"Is that who I think it is?" the unmistakable voice of Josh "the bear" Thompson calls out. My sister's sweetheart, my annoying little brother-in-law-to-be, stands by the baggage claim with a big sign in his hands. But there's nothing little about him. At six-foot-four and built like a football player, he could scare anyone. Except for me. I saw that boy in diapers, so he's still my annoying neighbor.

"One and the same," I reply, walking up to him, extending my hand.

"Son of a motherfucker, what kind of bullshit is this?" he says pointing at my hand. "That's not how we greet family; you know that. Come on. You know what's coming."

"No! Don't you dare, Josh. I mean it. Don't you dare!" I warn him, but it's no use. There's a glint of mischief in his eyes. I'm in for it now.

"Get her, Pookie Bear!" my sister calls out, joining us.

"Marni, no! We're in public!" I start to back up, while keeping my hands up. He drops the sign, his arms opening wide, giving me my cue to run. I make a weak attempt to get away, but these tall heels are no match against him.

"Pookie Bear Hug!!!" In one big swoop, he turns me around and into his arms, squeezing tight to the point I'm gasping for air. Everyone in the airport is looking at us curiously, and I'm instantly reminded of my family's need to show affection. Josh, having grown up with us, is no different. It feels foreign. I can't remember the last time I've had a hug from someone.

"Okay, you all had your little fun. Now, let go of me."

"Not until you say you've missed Pookie Bear!" Marni eggs on.

"The only missing there'll be is two balls when I kick Pookie Bear. Let go of me!" I demand, bending my knee as proof that I'm serious.

"There she is! The real ball-busting Cam-Cam. Let her go, sweetie. I need to give my favorite sister a hug."

"I'm your only sister," I correct her. "Now, let me get a good look at you." I take her hand then stand back so I can take in all of her. Wow, my sister had grown. She'd just graduated high school when I left here, but now, she's a woman. Confidence and sass radiate from her. I missed seeing her come into her own, but no more.

"Gosh, you look gorgeous, Marni. Radiant like the sun! And oh my God, the braces are gone!" I squeal.

"Yup! It was the summer after you left. I jumped for joy when they came off. Kind of wanted to kick your ass, though. You promised we'd eat candy and watch makeover shows the day it happened."

"Well, I'm here now for good."

"Eek! Really?"

She grabs my other hand in hers and starts jumping up and down, forcing me to do the same.

Marni hasn't changed a bit, her excitement always getting the best of her. I really did miss the brat. Letting out my inner Harley sister, I shout with her.

"Harley shake?"

"Do you even remember how?" She cocks a brow, doubting me.

"Psssh. I came up with it," I quip getting in position. "Ready, okay! Harley sisters, here we go!" I shout, once again getting all the attention of the airport attendees.

"Soouwweeeee!" Marni gives the go. Josh cheers us on while we complete the complicated handshake we perfected long ago. It was our calling card right before we got ourselves in trouble, but we gave no shits.

We successfully complete most of it until we get to the part where we hinge our legs together and skip in a circle. My heels give me a disadvantage, and we get tangled. We land on our asses, laughing hysterically. Josh helps us up, and we head out before the security comes to escort us away.

Arriving at the house almost two hours later, I'm exhausted. We live pretty far from the closest airport, and I'm running on no sleep in the last twenty-four hours, but I'll sleep later. I still have to survive the rest of our family. They'll give me hell once they see me, given how long I've been away.

As Josh parks his truck, I'm greeted by the sight of Uncle Joe in a speedo, on a dirt bike, getting ready to jump a ramp. My poor dad is running after him while my cousins are all on the other side waiting to see their father undoubtedly hurt himself. Anyone else would be surprised by this behavior on a Tuesday before noon, but not the Harleys. Joe is the family's crazy uncle, and for all his eccentricities, we can't help but love him. I've lost count of how many times he's landed in the ER. The man is a real-life *Jackass Show*.

"Just let him go, Richard. If I'm lucky, this is the one that cuts his dick off, balls and all," my Aunt Paula calls out from her porch.

The woman has been married to Joe since they were both eighteen. She takes all the craziness with a grace no one else possesses.

"Go, Joe, go!" I yell out, gathering the attention of everyone, including Joe, as I exit the truck. He spirals out of control, missing his jump, but somehow manages to straighten himself and stick the landing proving he has more lives than a cat.

"Surprise!" Marni yells as everyone gathers around. "I didn't want to say when she was coming in case she couldn't make it."

I'm lifted up by all my cousins, who are covered in dirt, and I can't be happier. These little gremlins were just little kids when I left, and they're teenagers now.

Once they put me down, my father comes over and pulls me into his arms, holding me tight. His quiet sniffle tells me without looking he's trying to hold back tears. I do the same. I can be strong. When my mom comes to the door, I put on my poker face. With her hands on her hips, glaring at me, I know I'm in deep shit.

"If it isn't the royal kiss-ass. That boss of yours finally let you out of the cage?" she asks, tapping her foot incessantly in the wooden porch.

"Something like that. You gonna just stand there acting tough or you gonna greet your pride and joy?"

"Get your ass over here before I knock you into the middle of next week looking both ways for Sunday!" she says, opening her arms to me. I make a run for it, lifting her in a hug as if she weighs nothing. She's a hundred-and-ten pounds soaking wet, having always been tiny and shorter than all of us. Not that it stops her from instilling fear in all of us. Everyone knows my six-foot-three dad is the big softy in the family. Seeing those two walking down the street is always hysterical.

"Don't you ever take that long to come home again," she reprimands as I put her back on her feet.

With all the wedding plans we have to make in a few days' time. dinner comes up before I know it. Like me, Marni is prepared and organized. She already has everything picked out. Truthfully, she's been ready for this longer than Josh can even imagine. Her big book of ideas all highlighted. Tomorrow, we'll start making calls and setting up everything. Money wasn't an issue since our family is wealthy, but that only gets you so far. I just hope this town is ready for how crazy it is about to get.

When everyone finishes dinner, I venture into the kitchen to help my mom with the dishes.

"You don't have to do that, sweetheart. I got it." She wipes her hand on the colorful apron she made herself.

Waving a dismissive hand at her insistence, I turn on the hot water. "I haven't helped in ages. Besides, I've got a lot on my mind, and you could use the help."

She comes over to me, her back against the counter so she can face me. I know it's coming. The hard questions. "Does the queen know you're here?"

"Probably." I shrug as if it's no biggie. At the moment, I really didn't want to have this conversation. Now that it's night and the distraction of my family is no longer there, all I can think of is her. Thankfully, my mother takes the hint and pats my back, leaving me to my own thoughts.

While I'm happy to be back, I also miss Helena. My previous assumption that I'll be okay is faltering. By now, she knows I left since I gave Delci specific instructions. I also left the royal phone behind. I came home with one suitcase, wanting to remove as much as I could of that former life. Too bad, that isn't helping my heart. It still beats wildly for her.

Did you miss me, Helena?

Chapter Four

~ Helena ~

"Delci, why didn't I get any breakfast this morning?" I call down to the kitchen, already irate with this day that's just begun. Cameron is still throwing her fit, it seems, since she hasn't reported back to the office. One more hour. That's all I'm willing to wait. My body is already having withdrawals from not seeing her. Last night, I practiced as much self-control as I could to not demand she come out of her room and talk to me. Even this morning, when her side of the hallway still remained dark, I bit my tongue. Well, I've had enough. She's throwing a tantrum.

"I didn't get an order in," Delci says dryly, taking me by surprise.

Has everyone gone mad in this house?

"Cameron and I had a disagreement. I'm sure she forgot to put it in. That's never been a reason for you not to send my standing order."

A scoff comes from the other end of the line. "A disagreement? That's putting it mildly, considering she left for good. Quite frankly, if I didn't need this job, I'd leave, too. Do with that what you want."

"Wait, what are you talking about? Cameron is in her room." I get up, already heading toward the hallway.

"Oh, sweetheart," she says, taking a long pause before continuing. "Cameron left yesterday afternoon. She was on the first flight out this morning. I drove her to the airport from the hotel she stayed at last night."

My phone drops from my hand, shattering on impact, just like my heart. This can't be happening. Running to her door, I turn the handle and discover it's unlocked. The room is empty and devoid of signs she's been in here at all. All her things are piled neatly on the bed with a note to donate them. My fingers run across it, the ache inside me growing. If only I'd been more insistent yesterday, I could have halted her departure.

The woman I've loved for years is gone. My cruel words ruined what little happiness I take from our time together.

A sob pulls from deep in my chest, as tears flow down my cheeks. I never cry. It's been ingrained in me that it's a sign of weakness. None of that matters now, though. I welcome the tears as they burn into my flesh. It seems I've always had a weakness after all… Her.

How long can I really survive without Cameron?

* * * *

Forty-two hours. That's how long it took for me to lose my mind. Honestly, I lost it four hours in. Every inch of the palace reminded me of her. The other thirty-eight, I was held together by the thin thread of the plan I put in place. With the help of Delci, Lorenzo, and a few, less than gracious characters, I was on a private jet to the US. I'd flown into a small airport in the middle of nowhere then was dropped off in a downtown area that had one traffic light.

This wasn't the America I'm used to visiting since I was young. I figured there'd be taxis everywhere, and I'd hitch one to her address. Fat chance. My lovely American escorts were eager to get rid of me, considering the liability I represented.

Now, to make matters worse, I'm pretty sure a storm is brewing by the looks of the sky. It's dark although it's barely midday. My heavy feet drag across the pavement as jetlag invades every part of my senses. Nonetheless, I have one mission. Get to my Cameron.

"Ma'am, are ya lost?" an older gentleman, standing on the corner of the street, in worn out jeans, asks me.

"A little bit," I admit, getting closer. He looks harmless, albeit a little confused when he takes me in. I'm pretty sure my designer slacks and top don't exactly mesh well here, considering everyone else is in jeans and casual shirts. I really should have dressed down for this, but I want to look nice when Cameron sees me again.

"Who ya lookin' for?" He tips his hat up to get a better look at me. The slow drawl makes him a real-life cliché of what I've imagined a cowboy to be.

"I'm looking for Cameron Harley, but I've lost her address. Do you know who that is?"

He laughs loudly as he slaps his knee. "Who doesn't know the daredevil Harley. I heard she was back in town, but I didn't believe it."

Daredevil Harley? There's no way we're talking about the same woman. The *Harley* I know is far from a daredevil. Pencil pusher maybe, but not a risk taker.

"That's okay. I'll keep asking. I don't think that's who I'm talking about." I smile politely, and start to turn away.

"She's about yay high," he says, pointing to his shoulders. "With big brown eyes, chocolate locks that cascade down her back?"

So far, he's batting a hundred, but how many women fit that description?

I tell him as much when he stares at me, waiting for my answer.

"Okay, okay," he says, realizing his vague description. "She's got a rose tattoo on her thigh. I should know. My son did it. Her parents almost had a cow over it."

A little confused at the meaning of *having a cow*, I don't ask, but he knows my Cameron. I'd discovered the tattoo one day when she was changing. It looked so sexy on her thigh that I never did forget it. "Oh, thank God, yes, that's her! Can you take me there?"

"I can get you close, but the Harleys are a protective bunch. Ain't no one getting on that land unless they like you," he says, pushing himself off the wall. "And you don't look like the type. No offense."

"What type is that, if you don't mind me asking?"

"City folk, although I can't quite place your accent." He motions me to follow him and leads the way to a beat-up truck parked close by.

"An accent? I don't have an accent," I reply. "One could argue you do."

"If you say so, Darlin'. So, what's a pretty peach like you, dressed to the nines, want with the Harley girl?" he asks, opening the door for me to get in. He doesn't move until I buckle my seatbelt.

"She left something behind in Jegan—where I'm from, by the way. I've come to return it." Instinctively, I rub the ring hanging from my necklace. It's a bad habit I have whenever I'm nervous. The ring is the only thing I have left from my maternal grandmother, who was so different from my own mother who'd married my father, the king, for money. The day she'd left home she completely forgot about my grandmother.

Not me. I'd visited her religiously until she died a couple months before I took over the country. This ring is the only thing I have of hers, since my mother got rid of everything else the minute she passed.

"Must be something mighty big for you to travel all the way from there. Jegans aren't known for traveling outside their land." He surprises me with the little-known fact.

"You know where Jegan is?"

"Yup, I'm a geography buff. Small country, rich in resources, and has a newly appointed queen." He eyes me curiously.

I let my hair fall over my eyes, trying to shield my face and look towards the window. I can't have my cover blown right now. Not before I get to her.

"Don't worry, your secret's safe with me. We don't go snitchin' around here."

I give him a weak smile, staying quiet the rest of the way and concentrating on the storm that starts to come down hard against the metal of the vehicle. Despite his advanced age, the man maneuvers the truck through the low visibility better than I ever could. If this is the way to Cameron's, she lives deep in the country. Not many houses surround the area.

The deeper in we go, the more I start to second guess taking a ride with a strange man. It would be just my luck to end up dead, like one of those episodes of *Forensic Files* Cameron got me addicted to watching. That didn't happen in my homeland. Panic starts to rise in me, and I already see my body in a shallow grave.

"Ya okay there? You look about ready to quake in your boots," he says, taking his eyes off the road for a moment.

"What?" I ask, confused.

"Sorry, forgot you ain't from around here. You look scared shitless. Is that better?"

Recognizing the saying from the many times Cameron used it, I chuckle. "Yeah, sorry, Cameron has me addicted to the American crime shows. I started thinking about how people end up dead after taking car rides with strangers. No offense, but I already pictured my grave."

"I'd be more offended if you didn't have that thought. I hope I'm still able to instill some fear, although my wife woulda killed ya first if she knew I had you in my car. The woman has a jealous streak."

His conversation puts me back at ease. We talk the rest of the way until we come to a stop along a fence. Up at the top is a sign announcing the entrance to Harley Ranch, the name enclosed between the imprint of two horses.

"Well, Darlin', we're here, but it's pouring really hard. I don't mind calling them, so they can come up and unlock the gate. It's a good mile up the road before you reach the main house."

"No, thanks, you've done enough. Besides, I kind of want to surprise her." I pull out a couple hundred to give to him for the trouble, but he refuses.

"It was my pleasure. Just make sure to come tell an ol' man the rest of this story one them days ya free. I enjoy adding to my geography trivia, including Jegan." He winks before taking off.

I wait until I can no longer see his lights then slip between the gap of the split rail fence. With the wind blowing hard against me, I'm thankful I brought my suit jacket. Although, it doesn't help much.

After what feels like forever, a couple houses come into focus through all the rain. I'm so excited to see them, I miss the rock in front of me and trip right into a pile of mud.

So much for looking my best.

I'm drenched, covered in dirt, and I'm pretty sure there's a small branch tangled somewhere in my hair. Eventually, I make it all the way to the door of the main house. Knocking on it quickly, I hope someone will answer. My teeth start to chatter, and I hug myself, needing a bit of warmth.

Suddenly, the door flies open, and in front of me is a thicker, blonder version of my Cameron. I've made it.

"Y'all come 'ere. We got a trespasser!"

Chapter Five

~ Cameron ~

"Cam-Cam, you gotta come see this! It's some lady saying she's your boss. A queen or some shit," Josh yells from the bottom of the stairs.

What!

I rush to the door, and my jaw drops. Helena is standing in the middle of the storm, drenched head-to-toe, in her favorite outfit. There's no way that will be saved. No amount of dry cleaning will fix the damage. I'll have to call the tailors to come out and try to recreate it. That's when it dawns on me. I'm not in Jegan. I'm home, and she is here. But that's impossible. There's no way she left the palace without guards. Unless…

"Do you know this lady?" Josh asks me.

I nod, unable to mutter out the words. My breathing constricts in my chest. She's here, but why? I don't dare breathe hope into my already broken heart. For all I know, she came after me because she needs a file or some information. That's plausible, right?

"Cameron, we need to talk," she states, her eyes burning with a fire I haven't seen before. When I mouth *yes*, she follows me inside.

Behind us, my sister and her fiancé murmur loudly. It can be heard throughout the house, probably alerting the others. Those two aren't good at being discreet, and sure enough, my mom comes in from the kitchen. Her eyes go wide when she sees Helena. My dad is right behind her, and he looks between me and her. Letting out a low whistle, he retreats to the living room. My mother does not.

She's about to kill us.

"Cam, a word please," she says, her eyes pointing daggers at me. She turns a sweet smile over to Helena. "Pleasure to meet you after all these years. It's always nice to see the person responsible for keeping my daughter away for five years. The guest bathroom is upstairs. Marni will show you the way."

"Mom, I don't think—"

"Cam, I said a word. In the kitchen now!" she commands, leaving no room for arguments.

"Go. I could use a bath. We'll talk after," Helena says, squeezing my hand.

Torn, I struggle to leave her side. I've tried to keep it together, telling myself I've been fine without her the last couple days. Now, I'm not so sure. Seeing her in my home, looking every bit as beautiful, even covered in dirt, I'm a slave to my feelings for her. *I love her. I can't change that no matter how many miles I put between us.*

"Fine, I won't be long," I reply then ask Marni to pull out one of my outfits for Helena to wear.

In the kitchen, my mother is pacing the floor, her displeasure coming off her in waves. I tap on the side of the wall, letting her know I'm there.

"Why didn't you tell me?"

"Mom, I really didn't know she'd show up here," I reply honestly.

"No, Cam. Why didn't you tell me you're in love with her?"

"What are you talking about?" I argue, defiantly crossing my arms over my chest.

Coming closer, she puts her hand on my shoulder, her eyes boring into mine. I hate when my mother uses her intuition against me. Nine times out of ten, she knows what people are hiding. The tenth is just her being polite to those who can't take the truth. Being her daughter, I'm not one given that courtesy. She's taught us to take the bull by the horns and face life head on.

"Baby girl, I wasn't born yesterday. You love that woman. I could see it the moment I entered the room, and she loves you. Did you guys have a spat, and you decided to run?"

"Shh!" I curse, pulling her deeper into the kitchen. "I won't lie to you, Mom. Yes, I'm in love with her, but she doesn't know that. She's not in love with me. She's here because she's a control freak."

My mother laughs, not a soft chuckle, nope. This is a deep from her belly laugh, as she miserably tries to hold it together.

"What is so funny?" I ask, unamused.

"That woman is crazy about you. Do you really think she'd travel all the way to the middle of the US for an assistant? Don't get me wrong. I'm sure you're great at your job, but no assistant is that great. That woman is so in love with you, she wasn't willing to be without you."

"That's crazy, Ma."

"Nope, that's love. Get your shit together, and go talk to her," she says to me then stops me as

---

I head out. "But no leaving until after your sister's wedding. I miss you, Cameron. We all do. Five years is a long time."

"I know."

* * * *

Standing in my room with a glass of milk, waiting for Helena to come out of the shower, is torture. I grabbed it on the slim chance she needed it. Whenever she travels, it upsets her stomach. She swears a glass of milk helps all her ailments, even when there's no scientific proof of it. I've stopped trying to convince her otherwise.

I have so many questions I want to ask. The greatest being why she's here. My mother thinks it's love, but wouldn't the years we've worked together be more than enough time to say something? I'm also unsure I'm ready for those answers, the implications of them, and what it means for her, for us. Now that I'm home, I realized how much I've missed it. I want to stay here with my family, and that means having to say goodbye to Helena forever.

"May I come in?"

Turning on my heel, I find Helena leaning on my door jamb, her long legs crossed at the ankle. Her wet hair making her look more youthful than her thirty-two years. Almost approachable. Standing there, looking so relaxed, it's as if she belongs here. As if she's been part of this family all along. Looking down further, I admire her long legs in my shorts. They're a bit tight, being she's always been thicker and more athletic than me, but they look amazing on her. They hug her curves just right, giving life to all the fantasies I've had.

I push away the thoughts, and swallowing hard, I nod.

"It's a bit far from Jegan, don't you think?"

"I could say the same thing to you," she says in a low, raspy voice, closing the distance between us.

Her hands land on my hips as she lifts me, placing me on top of the bookcase against my window. Pushing my legs open, she positions herself between them. Her mouth is so close to mine I can feel her warm breath against it.

"I brought you some milk," I blurt out, not knowing what else to say.

"Fuck the milk. There's only one thing that'll make me feel better," she says against my lips.

"What's that?"

"You."

The glass of milk lands on my carpeted floor as her hand goes to the back of my neck. She fists a handful of my hair. When her lips land on mine, my whole body courses with electricity. I eagerly open for her, and our tongues meet. I'm lightheaded, needy, and completely at the mercy of her demanding mouth. I wrap my arms around her neck, pulling her closer. I want more. So much more. The heady feeling of bliss, knowing she's wanted me too, is indescribable.

We kiss until I'm practically climbing her, the need for air the only deterrent from completely losing myself in her. When we finally come apart, her blue eyes bore into me, shining darker than I've ever seen them. Her forehead lands on mine, but we both stay quiet, not ready for the consequences of what just happened.

It's as if we know, once we speak, we'll have to put all the truth on the table. *Are we ready for that?* Answering my silent question, she shocks me dead in my tracks.

"I've wanted to do that since the first day you reported to work. I thought I could do it, but I can't" she says then pauses.

"Do what?" I whisper, all my hope riding on what she'll say next.

"Lie to myself." She pulls away from me a bit, a soft smile taking over. "I love you, Cameron. It took you leaving for me to know I don't just need you by my side. I need you to be my wife."

Helena goes down on one knee, undoing her necklace and pulling out the ring hanging from it. Since I've known her, she's worn it, and I never dared ask about it. She engulfs my hand in hers. I'm fucking speechless. This is really happening.

"Oh my God!" Marni yells, coming to a stop in front of the door.

"Well, I'll be a monkey's uncle, double wedding!" Josh calls out beside her.

"Mind if I ask her first?" Helena smiles up at them before returning her vision to me. "My dearest Cameron, will you do me the honor of marrying me? Of dictating every day of my life from here on out? To warm me with your smile and keep me on my toes with that sharp tongue of yours?"

"But…" I stammer, not believing what's happening. If someone told me five days ago I'd be in my childhood bedroom with Queen Helena professing her love to me, I'd have laughed at the absurdity. Yet, here we are. My heart beats a mile a minute, telling me to say yes, while my brain screams *run*.

Chapter Six

~ Helena ~

My heart is beating so hard against my chest, I'm pretty sure I'm having a heart attack. Her lack of response is about to become my cause of death. Indecision plays in her eyes, making my nerves skyrocket to the point I may not be able to keep it together. Here I am, the queen of a whole land, reduced to a beggar. Which is fine by me. I'll beg every day until she agrees to be mine because I can't exist in a world where she and I aren't together.

"What about Jegan? We both know this isn't exactly kosher there," she finally says, tears welling up behind her glasses. "We can't do this. Oh God, your mother. She'll kill me. I'm gonna be sick."

"Hey, shh. Come on, calm down, Cam-Cam. Please, Baby."

The endearment feels so natural, so right, coming from my lips. It shocks her, too. A soft gasp leaving her lips, I gently rub her thigh with my free hand. She's only ever been this nervous when riding on planes, and I was always able to calm her. I can only hope it works now.

"As much as I want to say yes, we both know it can't happen." Her low voice as she looks away guts me. A tear falls from her eye that she quickly wipes away. I never want to see her cry, especially not because of me.

"Let me worry about that. Tell me, do you love me?"

"Yes! Of course, I do. I have for a long time."

Her acknowledgement of her feelings frees me from the chains I've carried for so long. My guilt over this attraction held like a prisoner, but no more. I refuse to put us back in that cage.

"Then that's all that matters. Let me worry about everything else. If you love me, and I love you, don't deny us a chance."

She takes a deep sigh, pressing her glasses up her nose. "I'm crazy for this, but yes. I'll fucking marry you."

I push the ring up her finger then get on my feet, pulling her into a tight hug. In the background, her sister and Josh are both yelling the news at the top of their lungs. It's followed by the patter of feet up the stairs.

"I knew it!"

"I know, isn't it great, Mom. We're gonna have a double wedding? Right, Cam-Cam?"

Burying my face in Cameron's shoulder, I kiss it gently. A double wedding sounds just right, especially since it will make her my wife before I had to deal with all the fallout from this decision.

* * * *

"Do you know where my fiancée is?" I ask, taking a seat next to Josh at the kitchen island.

"Yup, at The Bull," he replies as if I understand what that means.

"Okay, how about we let the foreigner in on the little secret?"

With a mouthful of corn bread, he tries to answer. He's a bit barbaric, to say the least, chewing with his mouth open, but to Marni he's her "Pookie Bear". There's nothing to compare him to, but he was a gentle giant. From the first moment I stepped into the house, he's been cordial, including me in all the small talks. When I don't understand what's going on, he offers to explain. He even tried to get me to go fishing with him yesterday, but the thought of hours, sitting on a pond with a rod, did not appeal to me. He didn't take offense, shrugging it off and promising I'd take him up on his offer someday.

"How about you finish that mouthful then tell me?"

"Gowd iea," he mumbles mid-swallow. "Sorry, they're having their bachelorette party at The Bull. It's the small bar in town."

"What?"

He shrugs as if it isn't a big deal. But to me it is. I just got Cameron to accept my proposal. There's no way I'm okay with her out there doing the crazy things. As I've come to learn, my Cam-Cam has a wild girl streak. Twenty minutes after I put my ring on her, the family insisted on a celebration. The choice? Mudding. I had no clue what that entailed, but I soon found out. While exhilarating, it really showed how much I didn't know about her. Before seeing it with my own eyes, I never would have associated the activity with her.

"So you're telling me you're okay with Marni being at some bar, doing who knows what?" I ask.

"Let me tell you a little story. It's called *A Guide to Keeping a Marriage Going*," he says, stroking his chin as if he's about to tell me something very wise.

Humoring him, I wait for him to begin. Hopefully, afterwards, I'll convince him to take me to Cameron. "Do you have a marriage I know nothing about or something?" I joke, but his eyes pop out of their socket at the implication.

"May your tongue turn to chard. If Marni hears you, I'll be a dead man. That woman dreamed I cheated once, and she came over to my house, pounding on the door, at two in the morning. My mother pulled me out by the ear to deal with it. Marni is small, but she's scrappy. She told me just how she was gonna cut my balls off because she dreamed I was dipping in someone else's river." He leans in, looking around suspiciously before continuing. "She wouldn't talk to me for a whole week. I almost didn't survive. Now, I bring her tea every night and make sure she falls asleep soundly before I even close my eyes. Happy wife, happy life. Those are the words to live by."

"Aha, and what does that have to do with the fact our fiancées are at a bar getting drunk and probably doing bad things?"

"It means we don't interrupt girl time, especially not Harley sister time. Besides, Aunt Paula and their mom went with them. They won't let things get out of hand. If you wanna make it here on Harley Ranch, then you abide by the Harley ladies' rules."

"That's right. Spoken like a true Harley husband," Richard, Cameron's dad says, coming into the kitchen and taking a seat, as well.

"Thanks, I'll keep that in mind. Although, we're not planning to stay at the Harley Ranch for too long. Most likely, we'll be heading back to Jegan in a week," I inform them.

The two guys look at me in shock before sharing a glance between themselves. Not liking the uncomfortable silence, I take a sip of my water. When neither of them says anything, I can't stop from questioning them. Josh rubs the back of his neck, clearly uncomfortable with the subject.

"Have you asked Cam what she wants to do?" her father asks.

"No, but it's what's bound to happen. She only came this way because we had an argument, but our life is there," I inform them.

Abruptly, Josh stands up, leaving without saying goodbye and seeming upset. When he does, Richard also stands, patting my hand. "I'm not telling you what to do. In the end, we'll support both of you, but remember, she has family here. She was glad to be home for good. Maybe, you need to ask her about that." With his warning, he walks the same direction as Josh.

The conversation triggers me to call back home. I've been playing houseguest too long, acting as if I don't have the responsibility of a whole country bogging down on me. Powering up the phone I've purposely kept off, it buzzes to life, hundreds of messages pouring in from Delci, my parents, and various other pissed off people.

Bypassing reading any of them, I call Delci's private line.

"Where the heck are you?" she cries.

"Sorry, this got a little complicated, but I'll be home by Monday. How's everything over there? I have to cancel the Easter dinner. Where's Lorenzo? I need him to create a diversion?"

"That's not happening. Lorenzo cracked under pressure and gave you up. Your parents are heading out midday. You've got hours before they get to you. The only reason they didn't leave before is they're trying to make it a casual trip. No one suspects you're gone, except for the staff. All efforts to keep your escape under wraps are in full force."

"Thanks, Delci. I'll plan accordingly," I say, ending the call.

I fling my phone across the room. It bounces off the carpet as another message comes in. This isn't good. Time's running out. Our marriage can't wait until this weekend. It can barely wait till morning. Pacing the four corners of the small bedroom, my pulse rises.

Cameron deserved so much more than an impromptu wedding, but what other option do I have? I'll make it up to her once the dust settles, and I'll make sure we make it here with her family.

* * * *

The front door opens close to midnight, a bunch of screaming women making it through the door. Walking from the room I haven't left all day, I catch them just as they are coming in. The Harley women are in various stages of drunkenness. Paula is the most affected, and projectile vomits into the corner flower vase. Marni is riding Pookie Bear piggyback, kicking his sides as if he's a horse. Melanie, their mother, sways side to side, holding onto Richard on the way in.

The last to enter is Cameron. Though she's also intoxicated, she's tipsy at best, judging by her ability to walk in a straight line. Her gaze searches around, undoubtedly looking for me. I call out to her, and our eyes meet as soon as I do.

"Hey, baby. You have fun?" I ask, joining her.

"I really did. It's been a long time since I've done that." She envelopes me in a hug, her arms tight around my waist. She sways, humming a song as we slow dance to her beat. "You know growing up, I couldn't get out of here fast enough. I was so sure I'd become one of those porch sitters. I took the first way out of here. The royal ad posted on my school's job site just in time for my graduation," she says, her words slurring a bit. "was like a heaven sent. I was so wrong."

Maybe she's a little more intoxicated than I thought.

Her beautiful brown eyes mist, sending a pang to my core. The memory makes her sad. She really loves this place. It isn't right of me not to take that into account. Self-preservation pulls at me from one end. The innate need to protect her tugs at the other. Whatever choice I made, someone will end up a loser.

"Do you regret coming to Jegan?"

She considers the question for a moment, her eyes going distant. "I...don't regret meeting you." Her voice is barely audible, fearing I may be upset with her.

"That's not what I asked, Cameron. Do you regret coming to Jegan?"

Her silent nod as she buries herself in my shoulder is the final blow. All these years, she's lived a life she wasn't happy with.

"Please don't hate me."

"I could never, sweetheart. We'll take on this conversation in the morning. For now, just dance with me." I plant a kiss on her head, breathing in her scent.

"Okay. I can do that." Her body sways again. This time, no one hums, our bodies dancing to their own rhythm. Her steps are languid, exhaustion taking over as her soft body leans against mine for support.

"I think we should go to bed," I whisper. Agreeing with me, we make it to the bedroom in one piece.

Tomorrow is another day; I'll fix everything tomorrow.

Chapter Seven

~ Cameron ~

Waking up hung over this morning, I'm about to cry. My mouth tastes sour, and all I want to do is to bury my head in the covers. I'm not used to drinking the way I did at twenty-one. Two Smirnoffs and one Jello-shot, that's all it took to make me want to hurl this morning. It's shit, if you ask me. While I was the only one able to make it inside the door in one piece, I'm also the one with the splitting headache. The racket going on downstairs isn't making it any better. By the sounds of it, a small herd of animals is trampling all over everything. Probably, the wild herd known as the Harleys. I wanted nothing to do with it.

Reaching for Helena's warm body, I find she's no longer where she was when I fell asleep. Cool sheets that have been unoccupied for hours greet me instead. If she isn't here, then that can only mean one thing. She's been recruited for whatever shenanigans are happening below. I should be selfish and let her deal with my family. A day with them will toughen her up more than any of those Royal guard exercises she enjoys.

My soft heart wins in the end. I'll rescue her before they take her hunting or worse. My kin isn't above hazing the newcomer, and Josh is raring to go since he's the last one to join us. Most of it is innocent games, but Uncle Joe has a way of taking things too far, as do my cousins. Marni had to pretty much kill the last party when a firework misfired, and Josh burned his finger.

Damn it, I have to go rescue Helena.

I unwrap myself from the thick blanket that feels like heaven. Indecision hits me momentarily. My body begs me to just go back to bed. But I can't do that. Whatever is happening seems to be getting louder. Lord help us all. Placing both feet firmly on the plush carpet, I shoot up and immediately get dizzy. Lightweight isn't even the word for me. I am never drinking again. It's nothing a warm shower can't fix, though. I'm sure the chaos can wait another fifteen minutes. *Hopefully.*

Beating my personal best, I'm in and out and feeling refreshed in ten. I'd soak in a bath later — once I rescued Helena. If we're lucky, we can sneak off a little early from all the wedding insanity and indulge in a little fun in the bathtub. While we professed our love to each other, we still have to seal the deal. That happens tonight, because unless the world ends, I'm not accepting any interruptions. I'm having sex with my fiancée. Five long years without someone is long enough. It was the same for her. We are long overdue for a night of passion.

Fiancée. The word is still so foreign. Rubbing my finger over the worn ring, I love the feel of it against my skin. A token saying I'm hers. It makes everything official between us, and while I don't know the history of the ring, I know it's special. Back in Jegan, her mother would bitch about her wearing it instead of all the fancy jewels.

Shit. Jegan.

Last night's discussion finally comes back to me. How could I be so stupid? I practically admitted to regretting the past five years. She'll think I don't want to be with her. Ice burns through my veins at just the thought she might have left thinking I don't want her.

"I have to find her!"

Rushing down the flight of stairs, I come face to face with an empty house. Not a single person is in sight, but the ruckus is still going strong. Opening the door, I'm not ready for everything that hits me.

The first person I see is Aunt Paula doubled over gagging, and with just cause. Uncle Joe set off another of his stink bombs. I have to hold my breath to stop from gagging, too. Marni is beside her, laughing so hard she's holding her crotch doing the pee dance. It's similar to a bad slow-motion movie as I look from person to person. I glance left and right, but dust is clouding my vision from Josh riding in on his ATV. Squinting my eyes for a better look, I finally see what the whole commotion is about.

Marion and Ronald Payne are here, and they are pissed arguing with Helena. It's happening. The fairytale we've lived for the last few days is coming to a rapid end before it even had a chance to start. I march right over to where they are, needing to witness how my story ends firsthand.

"Are you on drugs? You're leaving a whole kingdom behind, so you can stay here with *her*? With these people?" Marion waves a dismissive hand toward my family, looking at them as if they're nothing more than peasants.

"These people have been kinder to me in the few days I've been here than you have my whole life. I guess it's good I called the press and gave notice of my official abdication early this morning."

"You did what?" both Ronald and I asked at the same time.

"I am stepping down. There's nothing in Jegan for me."

She can't be serious, yet she is. That tone in her voice means there's no room for discussion. Her rigid stance says she's ready to fight them on it. Guilt courses through me, but it quickly dissipates when she brings me to her side and kisses my hand.

"You thought this through, didn't you?" I ask, already knowing the answer.

"I did. When you opened up to me last night, I knew there was no other choice. I've loved you every single day you've been in my life. I'll love you every single one I have left. Jegan will be fine with or without me. I won't be if you aren't by my side. If your happiness is here at Harley Ranch, then here's where I'll stay."

Our sweet moment is interrupted by her father, who's had enough of us. "I'm very disappointed in you, Helena. You had what it took to be queen, and with a righteous king, you would have conquered everything. Consider us dead to you," he says, pulling his wife with him. They get in the limo and drive off, without a single glance back.

We watch as they leave, and everyone crowds around us. No one utters a word, giving us the silence we need to digest this. I can't imagine what Helena is feeling, but I want to comfort her. I'm afraid to move, to disrupt anything. She picked me over a whole kingdom, over everything, but at the cost of her parents.

"Their loss. They missed out on two amazing young women, but we welcome you with open arms," my dad says finally breaking the silence. He wraps an arm around each of us and kissing us each on the temple.

"We'll be inside, whenever you're ready," my mother says.

After the last of the Harleys make their way inside, I stand in front of Helena. Taking both of her hands in mine, I intertwine my fingers with hers. "You sure you made the right decision?"

"Yes, with every fiber of my being."

"So what now? You know it's gonna get tough here in a bit, right?"

She shrugs. "I'll become a Harley. Figure out how to be useful here and start over. We're still young. Who knows? I might still have a couple tricks up my sleeves. We don't need to have everything figured out. We don't even have to figure it out tonight."

"Ah, I beg to disagree." I pull her with me toward the house. "My family is about to leave for today's wedding hoopla. You and I have something else to figure out."

"Oh, yeah? And what's that?"

"You'll see."

Chapter Eight

~ Helena ~

A Month Later...

"Cameron! This is not what I thought when you told me to trust you!" I yell.

"Your highness, I think you'd better keep quiet. You've been very naughty, and naughty queens get spanked."

Five years I've waited to be with this woman, and within a month, she gets me to agree to some she-demon dominatrix thing. That first afternoon, after everyone left us alone for a good while, I'd finally been able to get my taste of Cameron. Her soft body writhing under mine as I took us both to the brink of ecstasy was the single most holy experience I'd ever had.

Her sweet pussy tasted like honey, and I'd quickly become addicted. I wanted more. I needed more. I lost count of the times I'd turned over to find her nectar during that night. It was a good thing we'd rented a room in town while an empty cabin on the property was fixed up for us to live in. I'm pretty sure everyone in town got an earful. We stayed out there for two weeks, after our quick Easter wedding, just enjoying each other company.

Since we'd said our vows, we've started getting to know intimate details about each other. Including, exploring our fantasies. I want nothing more than to give her everything she wants, and it's reciprocal. I like to think our sex life is pretty healthy. Being tied up, strap-ons, toys, you name it, we've tried it, even mild spanking, but that is about to change. In a sex-induced stupor, I said yes to her little surprise.

I never would have guessed she'd try to *Fifty Shades* me. It was cute at first, when I thought it was a joke. What harm could it be to indulge her a little bit. Neither of us has actually read the book, but we're pretty certain it involved some of the *naughtier toys.*

I'm not ready.

"What's the matter? Cat got your tongue now that I have you all tied up?" she says, coming closer. I can finally see her outfit in full, and I'm a bit scared, to say the least. She's wearing full-on Catwoman latex gear, and that whip in her hand does not look as if it's for play — or foreplay for that matter.

"Sweetheart, what are you wearing? That's not what I had in mind."

"I'm not sure, but Marni said I needed to get this, and this nice whip. I guess now we know why Pookey Bear is so docile." Demonstrating, she brings down the whip with a healthy amount of force. It lands against the bed between my legs with a loud whoosh, causing me to jump.

"I don't think this is safe, Cam-Cam. You know I love you, and I'll do just about anything for you, but this…this is too much."

"Relax, Marni said it's harmless. I even got the beginner's package. All it has is nipple clamps, a butt plug, and this small whip." She shrugs as if it's no big deal.

No big deal? When the hell did nipple clamps become a thing? What the hell happened to good old vibrators and magic wands to get adventurous. Sure, there are people out there who loved that stuff. Apparently, that included my sister-in-law who was as close to being my little sister as possible. I cringed at that thought along with the image of a bound-up Josh.

"Can we please stop talking about your family while any sexual activity is going on." My whole body shivers in disgust. "Can I at least have a safe word?"

"Pineapple."

"Pineapple? What kind of a shitty safe word is that?" I question, pulling on the ropes that have me attached to the bed.

"Well, I figure since you love pineapple on pizza so much, and it's a no-go for me. You say pineapple, and I know it's a no-go place."

"I don't know if this is some sick, twisted prank you Harleys are playing on me, or if you've actually lost your marbles."

"Silence!" she barks at me, lifting her whip and lands it right on my core.

"Pineapple, pineapple, motherfucking pineapple! What is wrong with you?" I yelp, pulling hard on the ties, but the stupid things don't come off. My area is burning, and I'm pretty sure it just dried up from that.

A frightened look fills her face as she realizes what she's done. It would be almost comical if I hadn't just gotten pussy whipped by an actual whip. Of all the places for it to land.

"Okay, so this is definitely not for us," she says, quickly untying me.

"You think?" I sit up on the bed, cupping my *flower* that's definitely wilted at the moment.

My upset wife comes over to sit next to me, wrapping her arm around my waist. I want to be pissed, but with her bottom lip pushed out and her puppy dog eyes I can't be. I kiss her forehead, and cuddle in close.

"Next time, before you decide to go *Mrs. Grey* on me, do you think you can let me in on it?"

"Yeah, I really wasn't thinking. I wanted to spice things up, but I should've known. I love our sex life, I just wanted to reciprocate. You always seem to be in charge, I was starting to feel like a pillow princess."

"Have I complained?" I ask, giving her my wolfish smile.

"No, but sometimes you gotta give up some of the control." She says grabbing the whip again.

"Hey, hey, no more." I grab the offending weapon from her hand. "Your days as a pussy whipper, are over. I promise to let you have a little more control if you never try this torture scheme again."

"Deal!"

"And you admit the pineapple belongs on pizza." I say laying her back on the bed.

"I rather be a pillow princess." She throws her head back in a laugh.

"Good, guess we got a compromise, now let's get you out of that death trap so I can get to my payout for all my pain and suffering. You on this bed for the next couple hours."

"I can live with that."

Epilogue

~ Helena ~

Five Years Later…

"Did you hear that?" I tap my wife on the shoulder when a gun pops off.

"Hear what, babe? Go back to sleep," she murmurs as she pulls the last small piece of my blanket off me then snuggles into my side. I married a cover stealer, plain and simple. Had I known that when I first asked her to marry me, I may have backed out. As soon as the thought crosses my mind, I call bullshit on myself. Cameron can steal every blanket in the world, leaving me to freeze, and I'd still have married her. She's my everything.

I lie back down, pulling my emergency blanket from under the bed. It will still end up wrapped around her at some point, but for now, I can bask in the comfort of it. Pushing away the sound that woke me in the first place, I close my eyes. My arms wrap around her tightly as I lay a soft kiss on her forehead. It's these little moments, that I live for. One thing is for sure; thanks to my Cam, I'm really living.

In the five years since I dropped everything to be with her, a lot has happened. I was disowned by my family and removed as the queen, of course. My dad took over, then my uncle a few months later. Cameron and I moved into the empty house next to my in-laws, and I started helping around the farm. I became a Harley and endured the craziness of becoming a legal resident, then an American citizen. No, ex-royalty didn't get a free pass. It was a humbling experience, to say the least. But it all ended up with the only thing that mattered. I got the girl, and a loving family by proxy. It had been a long road, but worth every hurdle. I snuggle in close as the memories of everything replay in my mind.

Bang! Bang!

The sound of the second and third bullets is unmistakable this time, making Cameron shoot up from her sleep. Her eyes go wide, looking at me for answers. I simply shrug, getting up. I get my bottoms halfway on when my wife lands with a thud on the floor and is unable to get up from the blankets that are wrapped around her so hard.

"Told you not to steal the blankets. You look like a fucking burrito."

"Shut up and help me. Through the good and the bad, remember? This is the bad. Get me the fuck out, so we can see what's happening."

"Fine but you need an intervention." I chuckle at how ridiculous she looks. I pull my pants all the way up then get her unwrapped quickly. Afterward, I dart out to the living room. As I do, a familiar knock resonates through my house. Josh is through the door before I open it all the way.

"It's uncle Joe. He's on the tractor, hollering at something and shooting. We need to go after him."

"Again? For Christ sakes. Cam hurry up before your uncle goes crazy on the foxes," I yell, not waiting on her. She'll follow us soon enough. Josh and I jump on the ATVs and speed toward the faint hollering we hear. Thankfully, it seems he's at the property edge and not in the numerous acres where it would take hours to track him down.

"Off the fucking property! We shoot to kill here!" Uncle Joe rambles, shooting another shot into the air.

This crazy man will get himself hurt or killed one of these days, trying to go after the wildlife that kept coming in at night. One thing's for sure. It makes for some entertaining days. Never a dull moment in the Harley residence. Right now, I'd settle for getting him back to his wife in one piece, or we'll be answering to her. That's a fate far worse than getting accidentally shot by Uncle Joe himself.

"Uncle Joe, stop! You know you can't see at night! Come back. Paula will be worried," Josh yells.

"It's not foxes! We got us some of those trespassers. It's happened. The feds have come for my moonshine. Well, they'll never find it! They'll never take me alive!"

"Fuck, in the fair chance there are people out there, we've gotta stop him!"

"I told you the government is watching," he exclaims.

Right at the end of the property, where the fencing meets the road, we catch up to him. Sure enough, there are people on the other side. Lights flash in our faces, and I have a feeling I know what this is about. A magazine called recently wanting to do a five-years-later article about Cameron and me, but I refused. The calls have gotten a little more insistent as of late, but this is uncalled for. I'll be making some calls in the morning, but that's the least of my problems. I need to get Joe away from them before they end up shot because of their intrusion. Josh and I climb off our ATVs to convince him to come with us. Seconds later, Cameron and Paula are in sight. Quickly, his wife gets him to obey her, and he follows her home.

Tomorrow will be bad.

* * * *

"How bad is it?" Cameron asks me, taking her seat at the breakfast table.

It was bad, and I've already gotten a phone call from my father reiterating how disowned I am. I still don't care what they think. I have my own little family here

"Well, the headlines are entertaining, that's for sure." Josh chuckles, sitting next to me and patting my back. "Our queenie here was apparently kidnapped and brainwashed by a pack of savage farmers."

"You're kidding?" Cameron's jaw drops.

"Nope and that was the nicest one."

He's always the comedian, but he's also my best friend. I ignore him and pour myself a glass of orange juice. "It'll blow over. I don't think TMZ is planning to run over here to find me anytime soon," I venture.

"Too bad, I was looking to get my fifteen minutes of fame," he says.

"Pookie Bear, you don't need fifteen minutes of fame. All the ladies would be after you. Can't have that. You keep your ass in this ranch, where no one can find you," Marni says, bringing over some pancakes.

"Yeah, Pookie Bear," I mock him. His response is to give me the finger. "You're right, baby. Can't have all these guns out there on display. Might make all the ladies faint." He flexes as he says it, and the whole table erupts into laughter, except for Marni who's steaming mad.

"Baby, I was joking. I promise," he begs, running after her when she walks off.

"We'll see how much of a joke it is when you're sleeping on the sofa. I've got BOB to take care of me." Her small feet move quickly, trying to add distance between her and Josh, but it's an uneven match. He catches up to her in seconds, lifting her up over his shoulder.

"Marni Harley-Thompson, don't you even think about it!"

Yep, life at the Harley Ranch is truly unmatched.

Looking for Another Fun FF Read?
Check out Playing For Keeps!

In the mood for a Paranormal FF Read?
Check out My Vampire Mate!

About the Author

Most days you can find Pixie running around trying to juggle 100 hats…one of which is Author. BTW, she still can't believe that's what she gets to call herself that. What started out as a passion for book blogging turned into publishing her very first novella… *Sealed With A Kiss.*

Pixie who is part of the LGBT Community, writes MF, MM and FF stories that are sexy, insta-love stories full of heart and with a HEA.

Her characters not only fall quickly, deeply, but are also possessive in nature. If she's not writing, then she's on Facebook…Tell her to get the hell out of there and get writing.

"Where Love Always Wins."

You can follow Pixie Chica via any of the social media by clicking the link below:
https://linktr.ee/pixiechica

Books by Pixie

Always & Forever Series
Sealed with a Kiss
In Plain Sight

Love Unexpected Series
Love at Sunset
Undeniable Love
Unleashed Love

Valladares Family Saga
Ivy's Rebellion

Tattooed Brides Series
Loved by Her
Loved in the Dark

Lancaster Falls Series
Because of Blue
Because of You

Holiday Hearts
Mistletoe
Undercover Santa
His Christmas Delivery
Stupid Cupid
Altared

Sweetville
Put a Ring on It
Stranded Christmas
Ring of Fire
Good Cop Bad Girl
Happenstance

Latimer Ladies
New Year's Kiss
Sweetness
Last Shot

Price Industries
Mine by Christmas
Give into Temptation

Sizzle Beach
Things We Did Last Summer

Standalones
A Wolfe's Ruby
A Royal Payne
Treat You Better
Teacher's Pet
Playing for Keeps
Curves Rx
My Vampire Mate

Box Sets
Holiday Hearts Collection
The Covingtons
Price Industries

9 798223 038405